Dear Parent:
Your child's love of reading starts here!

Every child learns to read in a different way and at his or her own speed. Some go back and forth between reading levels and read favorite books again and again. Others read through each level in order. You can help your young reader improve and become more confident by encouraging his or her own interests and abilities. From books your child reads with you to the first books he or she reads alone, there are I Can Read Books for every stage of reading:

SHARED READING
Basic language, word repetition, and whimsical illustrations, ideal for sharing with your emergent reader

BEGINNING READING
Short sentences, familiar words, and simple concepts for children eager to read on their own

READING WITH HELP
Engaging stories, longer sentences, and language play for developing readers

READING ALONE
Complex plots, challenging vocabulary, and high-interest topics for the independent reader

ADVANCED READING
Short paragraphs, chapters, and exciting themes for the perfect bridge to chapter books

I Can Read Books have introduced children to the joy of reading since 1957. Featuring award-winning authors and illustrators and a fabulous cast of beloved characters, I Can Read Books set the standard for beginning readers.

A lifetime of discovery begins with the magical words **"I Can Read!"**

Visit www.icanread.com for information
on enriching your child's reading experience.

This 2011 edition was created exclusively for Sandy Creek by arrangement with HarperCollins Publishers.
HarperCollins Publishers® and I Can Read Book® are registered trademarks.

SUPER HEROES COLLECTION

Batman: Meet the Super Heroes
BATMAN, SUPERMAN, WONDER WOMAN, and all related characters and elements are trademarks of DC Comics © 2010.

Superman: I Am Superman
SUPERMAN and all related characters and elements are trademarks of DC Comics © 2010.

Superman: Superman versus Bizarro
SUPERMAN and all related characters and elements are trademarks of DC Comics © 2010.

Wonder Woman: I Am Wonder Woman
WONDER WOMAN, BATMAN, SUPERMAN, and all related characters and elements are trademarks of DC Comics © 2010.

Superman: Superman versus Mongul
SUPERMAN and all related characters and elements are trademarks of DC Comics © 2011.

ISBN 978-1-4351-3711-0

Sandy Creek
387 Park Avenue South
New York, NY 10016

Manufactured in China
Manufactured December 2011
Lot 11 12 13 14 15 SCP 10 9 8 7 6 5 4 3

An I Can Read Book™

Super Heroes Collection

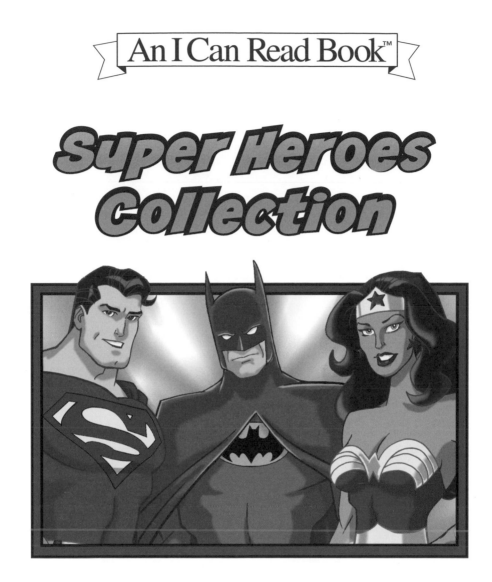

BATMAN created by Bob Kane
SUPERMAN created by Jerry Siegel and Joe Shuster
WONDER WOMAN created by William Moulton Marston

Sandy Creek
NEW YORK

TABLE OF CONTENTS

BATMAN™

Meet the Super Heroes

by Michael Teitelbaum
pictures by Steven E. Gordon

BATMAN created by Bob Kane
SUPERMAN created by Jerry Siegel and Joe Shuster
WONDER WOMAN created by William Moulton Marston

BRUCE WAYNE

Bruce Wayne is a very rich man. He is secretly Batman.

CLARK KENT

Clark Kent is a newspaper reporter. He is secretly Superman.

DIANA PRINCE

Diana Prince works for the US government. She is secretly Wonder Woman.

BATMAN

Batman fights crime in Gotham City. He wears a mask and a cape.

SUPERMAN

Superman has many amazing powers. He was born on the planet Krypton.

WONDER WOMAN

Wonder Woman is an Amazon princess. She is very strong and has a magic lasso.

The Gotham City Museum
was having a big party.

Bruce Wayne was invited.

Bruce spotted a statue of a dragon.

"That's an interesting statue," he said.

Bruce had never seen anything

like it before.

Suddenly, the dragon statue
came to life.

It flew into the air and shot
fire from its mouth.

People screamed and ran.

"How did this happen?"

Bruce said as he ran outside.

"I've got to stop that dragon!"

Bruce rushed to his big house.

Bruce had a secret.

Bruce Wayne was Batman!

Batman raced back to the museum

in the Batmobile.

The dragon flew over the city.

Gotham was in danger!

Batman took a Batarang
from his Utility Belt.
He threw it at the dragon.

The Batarang was hooked to a rope.

The rope wrapped around the dragon.

"Now I've got you!" Batman said.

The dragon bit through the rope

with large, sharp teeth.

Then it swatted Batman away

with its tail.

The dragon was too strong for Batman.

"I can't stop it alone!" Batman said.

"I have to call for help!"

Batman grabbed his sonic-wave device.

It gave off a high-pitched sound.

Only one man could hear it.

At the Daily Planet building,

Clark Kent's super-hearing

picked up the signal.

"Batman is in trouble," Clark said.

"This is a job for Superman!"

Clark changed into his costume.

"I'll have to fly at super-speed

to get to Gotham in time," he said.

Superman got to Gotham

a few minutes later.

"Batman, what happened?" he asked.

"I'm not sure," Batman said.

"But that dragon is dangerous!"

24

"I'll use my super-strength
to stop that dragon,"
Superman said.

Superman flew up to the dragon
and grabbed its tail.

The dragon shot a blast of fire
at Superman.

"The dragon must have been brought to life by magic," Superman said.

"My powers can't stop magic, but Diana's can," he said.

In Washington, DC,

Diana Prince's phone rang.

It was Batman.

"I'll be right there," Diana said,

"as Wonder Woman!"

Wonder Woman took off
in her Invisible Jet.
"Statues don't just come alive
and breathe fire," she said.
"This sounds like evil magic!"

A few minutes later,

Wonder Woman joined her friends

in Gotham City.

"I have a plan," Batman said.

He explained it to the heroes.

Superman and Wonder Woman

sprang into action.

Batman got out his steel Bat-cable.

Wonder Woman threw her magic lasso
around the dragon's jaw.
It weakened the dragon.
Batman used his steel Bat-cable
to pull it to the ground.

Superman used his freezing breath

to hold the dragon.

"That should cool you off,"

he said.

"Now what?" Batman asked.

"I can link minds with the dragon,"
Wonder Woman said.

"I can try to get the dragon
to reject the evil magic."
Wonder Woman reached into
the dragon's mind.
Then the dragon vanished
in a puff of smoke.

Batman, Superman, and Wonder Woman rushed into the museum.

The dragon was once again a statue.

Batman's plan had worked!

"Nice teamwork!" he said.

"Thanks to you two,
Gotham is safe again,"
Batman said.

"Thanks to us all!" said his friends.

I Am Superman

by Michael Teitelbaum
pictures by Rick Farley

SUPERMAN created by Jerry Siegel and Joe Shuster

CLARK KENT

Clark Kent is a
newspaper reporter.
He is secretly Superman.

LOIS LANE

Lois Lane is a reporter.
She works for the
Daily Planet newspaper.

LEX LUTHOR

Lex Luthor is the
smartest criminal
in the world.
He is Superman's enemy.

THE FORTRESS OF SOLITUDE

This is Superman's hidden home. Many secrets about his life are inside.

SUPERMAN

Superman has many amazing powers. He was born on the planet Krypton.

Lois Lane sped past Clark Kent.

She was on her way out of

the Daily Planet,

where she and Clark worked.

They were newspaper reporters.

"Why are you in such a hurry, Lois?"
asked Clark.

"I'm writing a story," Lois said.

"What kind of story?" Clark asked.

"That's my secret!" Lois said.

Lois rushed up to the roof.

Superman was waiting for her there.

"Hi, Lois," Superman said.

"Ready to do the story?"

"You bet, Superman!" Lois said.

"I thought we could talk somewhere a little different," Superman said.

"Where are we going?" Lois asked.

"You'll see," said Superman.

Superman flew at super-speed
up to the frozen Arctic.
"This is my Fortress of Solitude,"
Superman said.

"The Fortress is my secret home,"

he told Lois.

"If you want to learn about me,

this is the best place to come."

"This giant key unlocks the door,"

Superman said.

He put the key into the lock.

"I use my super-strength to lift it."

Superman and Lois

entered the Fortress.

Superman used his super-breath

to blow the door closed.

"That's amazing!" said Lois.

Lois pointed at two statues.

"Who are those people?" she asked.

"Those are my parents,"
Superman said.

"My father, Jor-El,
and my mother, Lara.
They're holding a model of Krypton."

"Krypton?" Lois asked.

"Krypton was the planet
where I was born," Superman said.
"This crystal shows pictures
of life on Krypton."

"Krypton was different from Earth,
but it was my home," said Superman.
"Then one day my father learned
that Krypton was going to explode."

My father put me in a spaceship
and sent it to Earth
to save my life," Superman said.

"Earth's yellow sun gives me
my superpowers," said Superman.
"Even when I was a little boy,
I could lift a truck."

"Wow," said Lois.

"What else can you do?"

"I can see through things
with my X-ray vision," Superman said.

"And nothing can hurt me."

"Nothing?" Lois asked.

"Only kryptonite can make me weak," Superman said.

"It's a piece of my home planet. I keep it in this case so it can't hurt me."

Suddenly, an alarm rang out.

Lex Luthor's angry face

filled up the computer screen.

"I will rule the city!" said Luthor.

"Watch what will happen

if I'm not given complete power!"

"Metropolis is in danger!"
Superman said as he and Lois
zoomed out of the Fortress.
"I have to stop Luthor!"

Luthor blew up a building
as Superman and Lois arrived.
"The buildings are all empty,"
Superman said.
"At least no one got hurt."

"Metropolis is mine!"

said Luthor.

He blasted another building.

A piece of stone fell toward Lois.
Superman soared up to catch it
and then tossed it
safely away.

"I can destroy Luthor's laser
with my heat vision," Superman said.
Two red beams shot out of his eyes.
Luthor's weapon blew up.

Superman stopped Luthor's evil plot.

"Your days of making threats
are over!" he told the villain.

Superman gave Luthor to the police.

"Thanks for the story, Superman,"
Lois said when they returned to
the Daily Planet.

"I can't wait until Clark sees it!"

"Who's Clark?" Superman asked.

"Never mind!" Lois said.

The next day Lois hurried
into Clark's office.
She tossed a copy of
the Daily Planet onto his desk.

"Here's what I was doing
while you were just sitting around,"
Lois said to Clark.

"How do you do it?" Clark asked.

"That's my secret!" said Lois.

Lois walked out of Clark's office.

Clark smiled to himself.

"I have a secret, too," he said.

"I am Superman!"

SUPERMAN

Superman
versus Bizarro

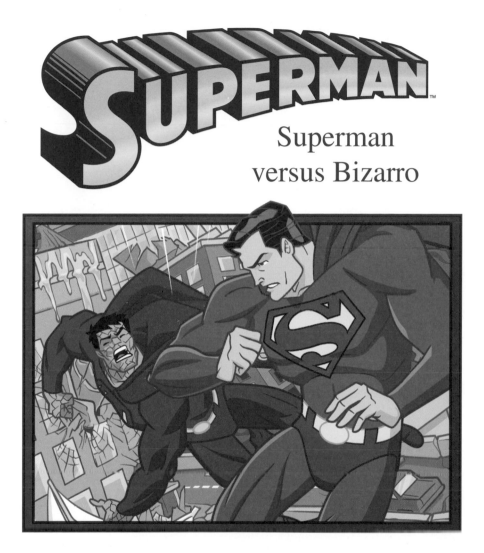

by Chris Strathearn
pictures by MADA Design, Inc.

SUPERMAN created by Jerry Siegel and Joe Shuster

CLARK KENT

Clark Kent
lives in Metropolis.
He is secretly Superman.

LOIS LANE

Lois Lane is a
newspaper reporter.
She writes a lot
about Superman.

BIZARRO

Bizarro looks
a lot like Superman,
but he has opposite powers.

SUPERMAN

Superman has many amazing powers.
He was born on the planet Krypton.

BIZARRO WORLD

Bizarro comes from a
planet called Bizarro World.
It is a lot like Earth, except
that everything is backward.

One morning in Metropolis,
Clark Kent was walking to work.
The streets were crowded and noisy
with the sounds of cars and people.
Clark heard something else.

Clark could hear a scared cat

cry from far away.

Clark stepped into an alley

and changed into his costume.

"This is a job for Superman!"

The cat was stuck high in a tree.

Superman swooped down to help,

but someone was already there!

Under the tree was a strange man.

It was Superman's backward clone!

His name was Bizarro.

"The kitty is scaring the tree!"

shouted Bizarro.

"Bizarro must save the tree!"

Bizarro grabbed the tree trunk

and pulled it from the ground.

CRASH!

Bizarro was powerful but clumsy.

"Bizarro is the best hero!"

said Bizarro as he flew off.

"I should follow him to make sure

he won't save anything else!"

said Superman.

Superman followed Bizarro
all the way to a burning warehouse.
"Bizarro will help the firemen!"
said Bizarro.

Bizarro lifted a fire truck over his head.

"Fire trucks put out fires!" he said.

"Wait!" said Superman.

Bizarro didn't wait.

He tossed the truck at the fire.

It crashed and exploded!

"Done!" said Bizarro.

Once again, Bizarro flew away,
but the fire was still burning!
Superman quickly blew out the flames
with jets of icy air.

"Does Bizarro think he's a hero?"
Lois Lane asked Superman
after he put out the fire.
"Yes," said Superman,
"but his thinking is backward
because he is from Bizarro World.
Bizarro must return to his own planet."
"Please make him leave before
he destroys Metropolis!" Lois said.

Superman heard new cries for help.

A boat was sinking in the river.

There was no time to lose.

Superman had to get there before Bizarro!

Bizarro was already at the boat.

"No problem!" said Bizarro.

"The river is hurting the boat,

so Bizarro will stop the river!"

Bizarro knocked down a bridge.

CRASH! SPLASH! WHOOSH!

Pieces of rock and steel

piled up high in the river.

Superman picked up the boat
and flew it to safety.

Now the river was overflowing.

It was going to flood the city!

With super-speed and super-strength,
Superman moved the rocks and steel
that blocked the river.
Water began to flow once more.
"Now to rebuild the bridge!" he said.

Superman used his heat rays
to weld the bridge back together.
Bizarro was angry at Superman.
"What are you doing?" he yelled.

"Bizarro is the hero,

not Superman!" Bizarro yelled.

Superman faced Bizarro.

"Bizarro, you can't stay on Earth!

It's time for you to go home!"

Bizarro stomped his feet.

The ground trembled and shook.

"No!" he shouted.

"Superman should leave Metropolis!"

Bizarro threw a statue at Superman.

Superman dodged the statue,

but Bizarro attacked again.

He shot freeze rays from his eyes.

Superman was covered in ice.

"Ha!" laughed Bizarro.

"Superman is not so hot anymore!"

Superman easily broke free.

"Bizarro, look around you!"
Superman pointed at the mess.
"You can't fix anything on Earth.
Your backward thinking is good
only on Bizarro World!"

Bizarro suddenly grew quiet.

He knew Superman was right.

"Bizarro is tired of Earth, anyway.

It is too backward here," he said.

"If I'm needed here," said Superman,

"you must be needed on your world."

This cheered Bizarro up.

"Bizarro is a big hero over there!"

he said proudly.

Bizarro turned and flew away.

He left Earth for Bizarro World

and the Bizarro people who needed him.

Back on Bizarro World,

a woman cried out.

"Help! Kitty is hurting the tree!"

Bizarro knew just what to do.

WONDER WOMAN™

I Am Wonder Woman

Written by Erin K. Stein
Illustrations by Rick Farley

WONDER WOMAN created by William Moulton Marston

My name is Princess Diana.

I grew up in a secret place

called Paradise Island.

I am an Amazon.

My mother is Queen Hippolyta.
She rules the Amazons
and protects Paradise Island.
All Amazons are strong warriors.

The Greek gods told my mother
about the dangers in the world.
Mankind needed someone
to keep the world safe.

The gods wanted to send the best

Amazon warrior to do the job.

The Queen had a contest to see which of us was faster, stronger, and braver than all the others.

Though I was a princess,

I did not want to become queen.

I wanted to fight for justice.

I secretly entered the contest.

I tried my best to win.

All of my arrows hit the target.

I outran all my Amazon sisters.

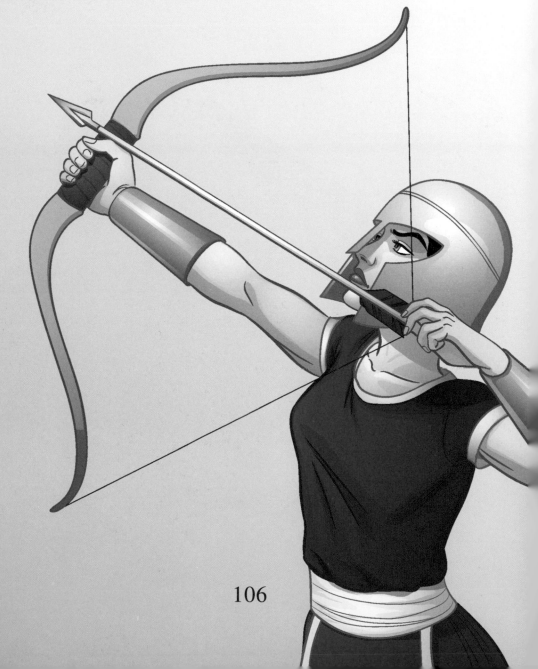

Our bracelets work as shields.

I moved as fast as lightning

to block all the arrows

fired by my opponents.

In the last sword fight,
I beat all the other finalists.
After I won, I showed my face
to the crowd.

My mother was surprised
but also very proud.
"Diana, you have earned it.
You are a champion," she said.

She gave me a special costume
and a new title to go with it:
Wonder Woman.

The Greek gods gave me

the ability to talk to animals

and a magic lasso

that makes people tell the truth.

112

To keep Paradise Island a secret,

I fly my Invisible Jet

so no one can see where I go.

I left Paradise Island
to live in Washington, DC.
My secret identity
is Diana Prince.

I work for the government at a top secret agency. At my job, I find out first when there is trouble.

ALERT: ROBBERY IN PROGRESS AT NATIONAL ZOO

ING!

CLASSIFIED

Two important reports come in.

An old bridge will collapse

the next time a train goes across.

And there's a crime at the zoo!

I spin very fast to change

into my super hero costume.

I rush to the rescue as Wonder Woman!

I fly through the city
faster than the speed of sound.
I use my super-strength
to help those in danger.

Just as the bridge collapses
I carry the train to safety.

There's no time to rest.

A tiger was stolen from the zoo!

Two strange men start to run.

"Stop!" I shout.

I toss my Lasso of Truth

and catch the robbers.

The lasso makes them tell me

where they hid the tiger.

Sometimes I have no choice
but to fight an enemy.

My friends Superman and Batman help
me train for all forms of combat.

Not every crime is easy to stop.

I must be prepared for anything,

even mythical beasts!

As Wonder Woman, I am famous.

My secret identity

lets me live a normal life, too.

Only my closest friends

know my secret. . . .

Superman
versus Mongul

by Michael Teitelbaum
pictures by MADA Design, Inc.

SUPERMAN created by Jerry Siegel and Joe Shuster

CLARK KENT

Clark Kent is a newspaper reporter. He is secretly Superman.

LOIS LANE

Lois Lane is a reporter. She works for the *Daily Planet* newspaper.

JIMMY OLSEN

Jimmy Olsen is a photographer. He works with Clark and Lois at the *Daily Planet*.

SUPERMAN

Superman has
many amazing powers.
He was born on the
planet Krypton.

MONGUL

Mongul is a powerful
alien. He wants
to take over Earth.

WARWORLD

Warworld is Mongul's
giant spaceship.
It is the size of a planet.

A giant spaceship moved quickly

toward Earth.

The spaceship was called Warworld.

An alien named Mongul

was in charge of Warworld.

Mongul was very powerful.

He planned to take over Earth.

Inside Warworld,

Mongul sat in his control chair.

"Soon this planet will be mine!"

he said.

At US Army headquarters,

Warworld appeared on the screen.

"What is that?" one general asked.

"An alien spaceship," said another.

"Prepare for an attack!"

At the *Daily Planet* newspaper,

Lois Lane stepped into

Clark Kent's office.

Clark was looking out the window.

"Stop staring into space,"

Lois joked,

"and do some work."

DAILY PLANET
EXCLUSIVE:
WHO IS
SUPERMAN?

SUPERMAN
RETURNS

But Clark wasn't listening to Lois.

His super-hearing had picked up

the sound of explosions.

"What's wrong?" Lois asked.

But Jimmy Olsen rushed in
before Clark could answer.
"An alien is attacking the city!"
Jimmy cried.

Clark changed in a flash.

"This looks like a job for Superman!"

he said.

Superman flew over Metropolis.

Below, he spotted Mongul.

The army was battling the alien.

But Mongul was so strong,

nothing hurt him.

A crowd of people ran in panic.

Superman spotted his friends.

"It's Jimmy and Lois!" he cried.

"They must be here to cover the story!"

Jimmy and Lois were standing

right in the alien's path.

"I have to save them!"

Superman said.

Superman grabbed his friends
just before Mongul reached them.
Soldiers came to help
as Mongul charged at Superman.
He pounded the Man of Steel
with his enormous fists.

Mongul caught Superman off guard.

"The first one's free, big guy,"

Superman said, getting to his feet.

"Let's see what you've got, puny being!"

Mongul roared.

Superman zoomed toward the villain.

SLAM!

Superman sent Mongul crashing

into a nearby building.

The building began to fall over.

It tumbled toward the crowd below.

Superman raced to the falling building

and caught it just in time.

"I'd better move this battle

to a safer place!" he said.

Superman began running

around Mongul.

He circled him again and again.

Superman ran faster and faster.

The Man of Steel created a

powerful cyclone.

The whirling funnel of wind

picked Mongul up off the ground.

Mongul went flying into space.

Superman followed Mongul into space. "Now I can stop you without anyone getting hurt!" Superman said.

"You cannot defeat me!" Mongul shouted.
The two powerful enemies clashed
in a cosmic battle!

With a blast
of his mighty super-breath,
Superman forced Mongul
back inside Warworld.

Superman used his heat vision
to destroy Warworld's engines.
KA-BOOM!

Using his super-strength,

Superman heaved Warworld far away.

It disappeared deep into space.

"That ship is on a one-way trip!"

Superman said as he headed back home.

Earth was saved.

Back at the Daily Planet building,
Lois entered Clark's office.

"And where were you when I was on
the story of the year?" Lois asked.

"Like you said," Clark replied.

"I was just staring into space."